P9-CEJ-169

1-20-99 Nh
BaT
15.95

When Sophie Gets Angry—
Really, Really Angry...

BY MOLLY BANG

THE BLUE SKY PRESS

An Imprint of Scholastic Inc. • New York

HAMPTON PUBLIC LIBRARY

HAMPTON 23669

Sophie
was busy
playing
when...

MY TURN

...her sister grabbed Gorilla.

"No!" said Sophie.
"Yes!" said her mother.
"It is her turn now,
Sophie."

Oh,
is Sophie
ever angry
now!

She kicks. She screams.
She wants to smash the
world to smithereens.

SMASH

She
roars
a red,
red roar.

Sophie is a volcano,
ready to explode.

And when Sophie
gets angry—
really, really angry...

She runs and runs
and runs until she
can't run anymore.

Then,
for a little while,
she cries.

tweet

Now she sees the rocks,

the trees and ferns.

She hears a bird.

She comes to the
old beech tree.
She climbs.

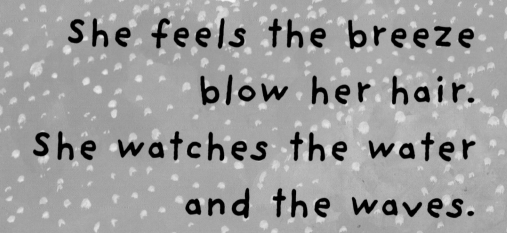

She feels the breeze
blow her hair.
She watches the water
and the waves.

The wide world
comforts her.

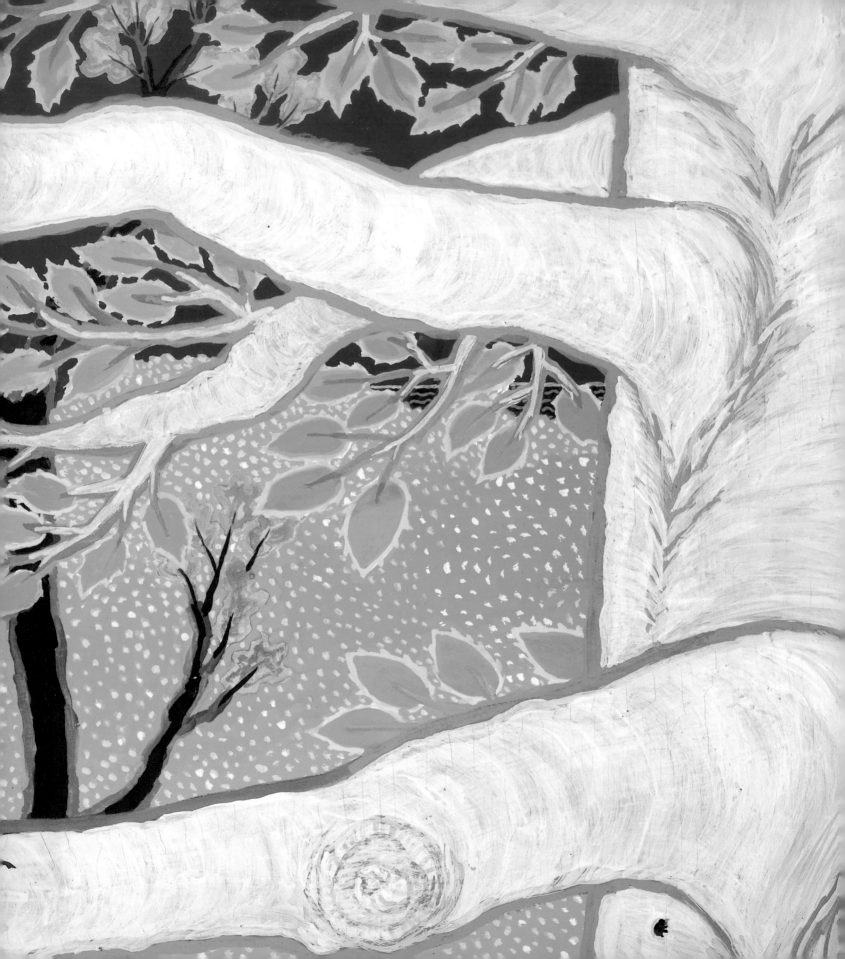

Sophie feels better now. She climbs back down...

...and heads for home.

I'M HOME

The house is warm and smells good. Everyone is glad she's home.

And Sophie
isn't angry
anymore.

PURR

HAMPTON PUBLIC LIBRARY

3 3245 0052 0212

NORTHAMPTON

WITHDRAWN

To all children, and to all moms and dads,
grandmothers and grandfathers, aunts and uncles and friends,
who ever get angry — even once.

M. B.

When Sophie gets angry, she runs out and
climbs her favorite tree.
Different people handle anger in different ways.

What do you do when you get angry?

THE BLUE SKY PRESS

Copyright © 1999 by Molly Bang
All rights reserved.

No part of this publication may be reproduced or stored in
a retrieval system or transmitted in any form or by any
means, electronic, mechanical, photocopying, recording, or
otherwise, without written permission of the publisher.

For information regarding permission,
please write to: Permissions Department,
The Blue Sky Press, an imprint of Scholastic Inc.,
555 Broadway, New York, New York 10012.

The Blue Sky Press is a registered trademark of Scholastic Inc.

Library of Congress catalog card number: 97-42209

ISBN 0-590-18979-4

10 9 8 7 6 5 4 3 2 1   9/9 0/0 01 02 03

Printed in Singapore   46
First printing, March 1999